To Sylvie's staff, particularly Alex—thank you!

BEACH LANE BOOKS
An imprint of Simon & Schuster Children's Publishing Division
1230 Avenue of the Americas, New York, New York 10020
Copyright © 2016 by Marla Frazee
BEACH LANE BOOKS is a trademark of Simon & Schuster, Inc.
For information about special discounts for bulk purchases, please contact Simon
& Schuster Special Sales at 1-866-506-1949 or business@simonandschuster.com.
The Simon & Schuster Speakers Bureau can bring authors to your live event.
For more information or to book an event, contact the Simon & Schuster Speakers
Bureau at 1-866-248-3049 or visit our website at www.simonspeakers.com.
Book design by Ann Bobco
The text for this book was set in Heatwave.
The illustrations for this book were rendered in black Prismacolor pencil and gouache
on Strathmore 1-ply cold press paper.
The display type was hand-lettered by Marla Frazee.
Manufactured in China
0816 SCP
First Edition
10 9 8 7 6 5 4 3 2 1
Library of Congress Cataloging-in-Publication Data
Names: Frazee, Marla, author.
Title: The bossier baby / Marla Frazee.
Description: First edition. | New York : Beach Lane Books, [2016] | Summary:
"Boss Baby used to be in charge of his family, but that was before he got an even
bossier baby sister"— Provided by publisher.
Identifiers: LCCN 2015045579 | ISBN 9781481471626 (hardback)
| ISBN 9781481471633 (eBook)
Subjects: | CYAC: Babies—Fiction. | Brothers and sisters—Fiction. | Humorous stories.
| BISAC: JUVENILE FICTION / Family / New Baby. | JUVENILE FICTION / Humorous
Stories. | JUVENILE FICTION / Family / Siblings.
Classification: LCC PZ7.F866 Br 2016 | DDC [E]—dc23 LC record available at
https://lccn.loc.gov/2015045579

introducing

the

BOSSIER
BABY

AS HERSELF!

by Marla Frazee

BEACH LANE BOOKS   New York   London   Toronto   Sydney   New Delhi

From the moment his baby sister arrived,

the Boss Baby had a feeling
that change was in the air.

The first thing the new executive did was outline her
business plan and restructure the organization . . .

from the top

down.

Then she demoted the Boss Baby and promoted herself to Chief Executive Officer, CEO for short.

The CEO was bossier than
the Boss Baby had ever been.

Which seems impossible.

Even so, the staff was strangely delighted.
The Boss Baby had never seen them so happy.

This made him miserable.

So did her perks.

There was the organic catering service.

Aromatherapy.

Stress management.

Afternoon spinning.

A full-time
social
media
team.

And, of course, the private limo.

The Boss Baby had
had some perks
in his time, but
nothing like this.

He was furious.

But the CEO and staff
paid no attention
to him.

No matter what he did.

Where he did it.

Or how outrageous it was.

Finally the Boss Baby just gave up.

He made no demands, had no fits,

exhibited no temper, and weirdly

had no opinions about anything at all.

This was highly irregular.

But the CEO knew what to do.

She wasn't CEO for nothing!

And at last the company was back to business,
operating productively, cooperatively, and efficiently . . .

most of the time.